one way

one way

HÉLÈNE HÉRAULT

TRANSLATED BY
LIZA TRIPP

This is a work of fiction. The characters and circumstances herein are products of the author's imagination and any resemblance to real places or people are merely a coincidence.

Originally published in French as Sens Unique
by L'Ire de l'Ours Éditions, Courpière, France.

"Juste une femme," lyrics and music by Anne Sylvestre.
Juste une femme, paroles et musique Anne Sylvestre Edition BC Musique.

ISBN: 978-1-971238-99-9 (paperback); 978-1-971238-98-2 (ebook)
LCCN: 2026934218
First Printing: 2026
Printed in the United States of America
Published by Silent Clamor Press, Los Angeles, CA

praise for hélène hérault

I had read Hérault's 2017 short story collection, *La Petite Prigent*, and was already a fan of her deft writing style. After contributing to an anthology, the author is now back on the publishing scene with this novella, which has certainly left its mark on me.

I have recently noticed a certain trend towards short texts. They can sometimes leave you feeling slightly frustrated, as if the author did not completely commit to their subject matter. Yet I certainly did not feel that way with *Sens Unique*, which is a testament to Hélène Hérault's powerful writing.

The novella begins in epistolary form, as Béatrice writes a series of twenty-four letters to Gaëtan, the husband she has just left. He has no way of responding—the letters have no return address. These one-way letters express in finely nuanced detail all of the (until now unspoken) resentment of this wounded woman towards the arrogant man who has held her emotionally captive. The second part of the book takes a hard turn towards tragedy. It's a quick read, because once you start you can't stop, and it's as gripping as it is moving. Once again, Hélène Hérault has won me over with her talent for choosing the perfect words without ever getting bogged down in useless digressions. This short yet powerful book was truly a delight.

LIRE EN VENDÉE, ÉCRIVAINS DE VENDÉE, TRANSLATED FROM THE FRENCH

Thirty-two years is a long time. Yet that is how long it's taken for Gaëtan (a harried CEO) and Béatrice (a fashion executive) to now split. Béatrice has decided to leave. And to write him letters. Letters to which has no way of responding, and which give her the chance to take vacation, discuss their daughter Clara, reconnect with Gaëtan's ex, and look back on their life together, which has changed over the years. Midway through, *Sens Unique* abandons the epistolary format, taking another narrative direction. That's the cunning side of this novella by Hélène Hérault (an alum of the *Lire Magazine* Workshops) who with her definitive mastery of the ellipsis, knows just how to surprise the reader.

JEAN HURTIN, *LIRE MAGAZINE*, TRANSLATED FROM THE FRENCH

Béatrice writes to Gaëtan. But Gaëtan doesn't answer her. It must be said that Béatrice has left their home for good, intentionally not leaving any forwarding address. "So this will be a one-way arrangement," and an analog one at that. No phone calls or emails. Nothing but paper. Because she has things to write and things to say, things to do too. And the accusations are coming fast and furious. Thirty-two years of shared life have left their mark, and there has definitely been some wear and tear, some fractures too. Yet it's as if everything were skewed from the start. To know the beginning, you'll need to wait until the end, and once you get there, you'll wonder how anything could have ever existed between the two of them. That's the power and edge of Hélène Hérault's *Sens Unique*. You'll compulsively turn the pages, gripped by whatever lies behind Béatrice's departure. Ultimately, you'll ask yourself how she's made it this long without imploding. Perhaps it's because while we'd like to know everything, sometimes we cannot explain everything. It's in the air—a sign of the times.

FRANÇOIS BRAUD, *BROBLOGBLACK* (SEPTEMBER 11, 2024), TRANSLATED FROM THE FRENCH

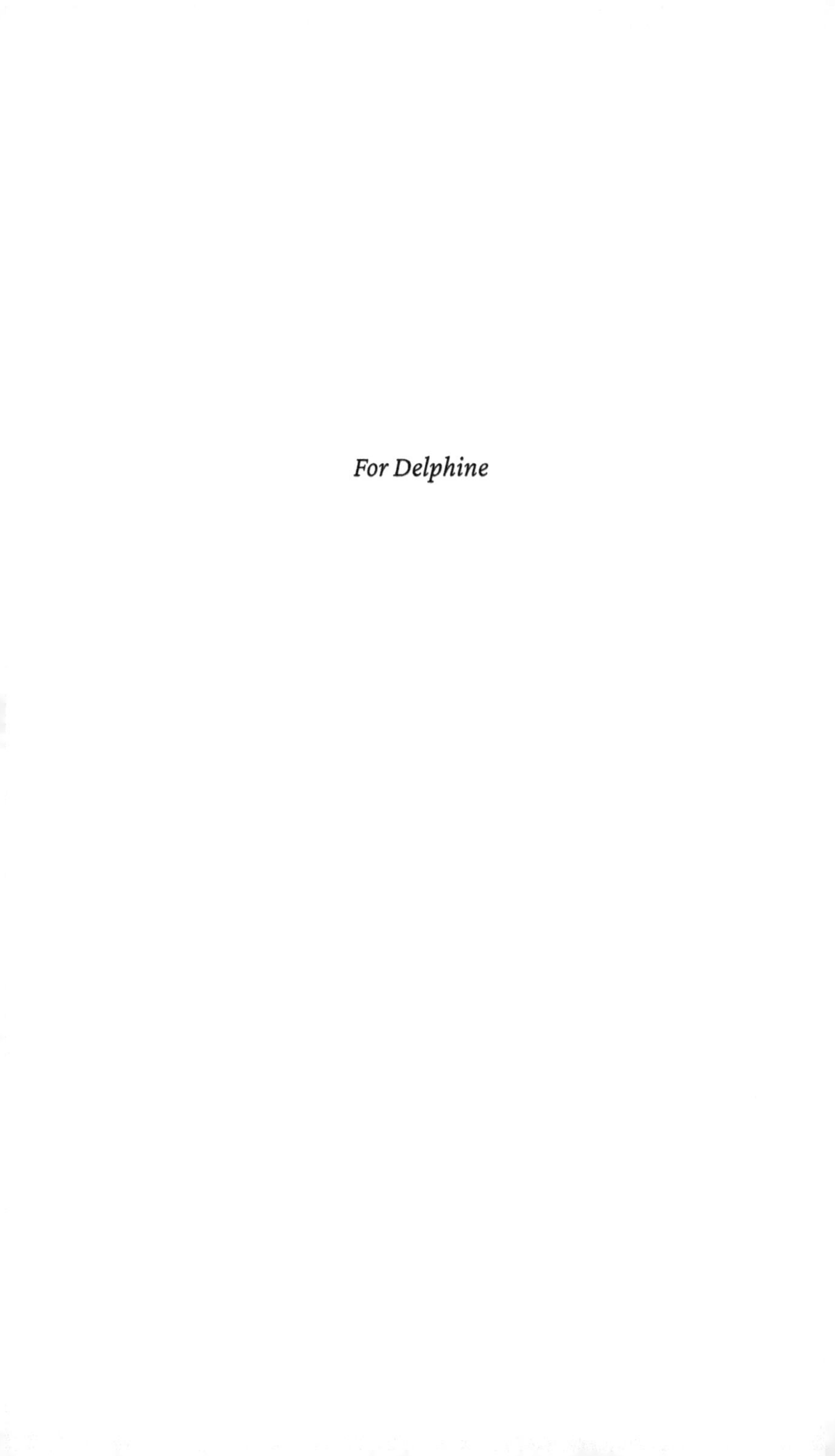

For Delphine

That's not a tragedy—
that's just a woman.

ANNE SYLVESTRE

contents

PART TWO

foreword

FRANÇOIS BRAUD

No one reads forewords. So it feels like I'm writing into the void. A confounding thought, right? Although maybe that hook nevertheless drew in a few sets of eyes. Hence my question. I'm waiting for your response. If you're still here, I've managed to convince you. Of what? That reading what follows is clearly worth the effort. Plus, foreword authors are super-efficient—I know how to do a good blurb. Worse comes to worst, I'd happily have you fly past this completely and dive straight into *One Way*, into these twenty-four letters Béatrice sends to Gaëtan, to settle (in epistolary fashion) a very old score.

Béatrice writes to Gaëtan with paper and pen, but Gaëtan cannot write her back. Note that Béatrice has left home to never return, purposefully leaving no forwarding address: "*So this will be a one-way arrangement.*" She communicates the old-fashioned way, using neither phone nor email. The former (too intrusive), and the latter (too immediate) would have allowed for conversation. Yet Béatrice needs to be alone; she needs time. Which rules out both of those modern communication methods in favor of what English speakers call, not without irony, "snail mail." The mail takes time. It requires you to wait (at least a day!), break open the seal (cleanly with a letter opener or messily with a finger), wonder who sent it, (unless you recognize the handwriting or read the name on the back), what it might say (there's no subject header like in an email), unfold the actual missive (there might be several pages), and decipher the handwriting (sometimes you need to be Champollion to do so). All that effort no one goes to anymore, or at least rarely.

Who writes letters these days? Well Béatrice does, and therefore so does Hélène Hérault, who brings her to life. Because both women have things to write, things to say—things to experience. You'll find the circumstances underlying Béatrice's departure gripping, and no doubt inhale the pages that follow. In the end, you'll ask yourself how time can flow so long without overflowing. Perhaps because we'd like to know everything, but sometimes not everything can be explained; it's something in the air. Does time have nothing to do with it? Well sometimes it does. Take a moment here—you won't be disappointed.

François Braud

translator's note

Hélène Hérault is a true craftswoman of language. In this noirish novella, she artfully manipulates the French language to powerful effect, exploiting its nuances and stretching its possibilities. By having her protagonist Béatrice take up her own pen, she triumphantly gives her the upper hand after years of living life in the background. She now has the ability to control how things will unfold, and her words at once convey a mixture of restraint, rage, vengefulness, and resignation, all cloaked in a degree of French *politesse.* This unique tone, with its simmering yet always controlled anger, gives the novella its remarkable tension and pacing.

Preserving that fraught tension was essential to recreating the experience of the original text in English. What words could Béatrice utter in English that would simultaneously allow others to remain unsaid? A change in language can certainly present some hurdles. While sentence fragments can easily be used to excellent stylistic effect in French, English requires a more traditional sentence structure to not be confusing. And while (at the other end of the spectrum) it is not unusual for a French sentence to extend the better part of a page, transposing that formula into English typically yields a baffling, chaotic sentence that makes its speaker come across as unhinged.

Yet while Béatrice grapples with some difficult, mixed emotions, she is always lucid. The translation needed to convey that wide range of emotion, while still reminding the reader of her stability. Indeed it is ultimately her mental strength and control that have allowed her to endure a situation that is all too familiar in so many languages.

Liza Tripp

part one

JANUARY 18,

MY DARLING,

(I'm strangely still attached to that cliché phrase).

It's the start of a new year, but really more like the start of a bad movie or an airport novel. Because by the time you read this letter, I'll be gone. I know—unoriginal, utterly unoriginal. It's been a few days, maybe more? I'll preserve the suspense and save you the long-winded speech about why I needed to leave. I've left, that's all. It's as simple and abrupt as that.

And now there you are, sitting perplexed and edgy in our empty house, faced with a fait accompli. You'll hate that, but there's nothing for it. It'll be a sudden blow to your pride and that visceral need you have to control everything. Rest assured, the fridge is full. As for everything else? You'll have to manage, or figure it out with Madame Grellier (reminder: she comes Wednesday mornings).

Enjoy your evening; I didn't take the TV. If there's a rugby match on, you can just tell yourself I went to bed early.

Béatrice

JANUARY 22,

GAËTAN,

Take this second letter as an (intentional) intrusion of your private life into your professional world. How many times did I have to suffer the reverse?

Let's set things straight right away: I'm going to write to you, regularly, and you won't be able to respond. A plain envelope, no return address. The Postal Service took the place of origin off postmarks a long time ago. You won't be able to contact me by mail or by phone—you can be sure of that. That would be too easy. And you've by now figured out that the same goes for emails. Oh—and leave Clara out of all this. Our daughter doesn't know where I am either.

So this will be a one-way arrangement.

I'll bear the risk. You can choose not to open these envelopes. But I know you. You'll want to know everything, control everything, like always. You're going to read my letters. You'll get annoyed, you'll get angry, but you're going to read every word I write.

So here's this letter, like an assignment on your desk. To put among your stacks of files, arranged according to priority, seriousness, disdain, or indifference. Everything meticulously laid out, classified. Except for this piece of mail—it bothered you before you even opened it.

This red envelope is ridiculous. Do you remember how red used to be our favorite color? I'm beginning to doubt that you do; the last scarf you gave me was green. But I digress. Above all, don't try to find out how you received this letter; your associates and partners (note the wording) will be useless here. Don't bother them with this. You can find plenty of other things for them to do without making yourself look like a fool over a private matter that could turn ugly for you.

Hang on to a bit of your dignity; avoid blowing your top and accusing everyone in your path. Here again, I'll take the risk, for other people this time. *Because they have done nothing wrong.* This letter is on your desk—that's it. And this mystery will become yet another element of your nebulous relationship with material concerns.

So let me repeat the rules of the game. You'll see they are really quite simple: I write to you, you read my letters, but you can't answer me. In reality, there are three of us involved, because life also plays its part. Consequently, neither you nor I know how or when the game will end. But I'll give you a clue, since I'm one step ahead. These letters will turn up at different locations. Not according to my mood, but depending on their contents. Consider that a necessary prelude.

Gaëtan, as you read these lines, sitting at your massive desk—actually you're probably standing up, nervously pacing the room after having requested (demanded) that no one bother you—at this precise moment, somewhere, I exist. As I have for thirty-two years. I don't only exist at night, late at night. I don't only exist on Sundays or during our rare vacations. I don't spend my days holding my breath waiting for you. I live, Gaëtan. I have a job, hobbies, a daughter, friends, a home. A life! A life you chose to ignore. Well it's catching up with you, right now. I'll leave it at that.

Enjoy your day; you'd better get back to work. Even though I've now invaded a little corner of your mind. But please don't go lashing out at any of the women working for you.

As for me, everything's going really well, thank you!

Speak to you very soon—between the lines.

Béatrice

FEBRUARY 8,

MY DARLING,

I'm having a good vacation. It's a change of scenery in the middle of winter—sea, waves, everything I love. It's nice out, I have time for myself. It's perfect.

Take care of yourself.

Béatrice

You have very few clues how to find me. That reminds me. The bank knows nothing, and you may have noticed that I'm not using the joint account.

FEBRUARY 18,

GAËTAN,

By this fourth missive, I imagine you've been able to detect some subtle differences in these letters. I write "Gaëtan" on the ones sent to your office, but reserve "My Darling" for the ones that go to the house. You'll never guess what happened to me. It was a little while ago, but "when" hardly matters. It was a little adventure that was as joyful as it was unexpected. I met some of your colleagues, your subordinates I should say, under circumstances that would be premature for me to tell you about. Very nice people. A little broken, but determined—full of fight. Some of the women are pretty great. We talked about a bit of everything, their schedules, the underwhelming or complete lack of respect, their paltry wages, the work environment. Truly very informative. Don't worry, no one knew who I was.

At this point, despite my efforts to reassure you, I can feel you're a bit nervous. Have you lost a lot of hair over the last few days? Perhaps you're agitated, irritable, bloated. I hope you're not wearing shirts that are too tight on you. How unfortunate if another shirt button were to pop off during a meeting. Self-control! Isn't that what you demand of everyone else?

Anyway, these meetings. Astounding. I didn't talk about you right then and there, but I'll definitively do so soon—and in detail.

Are you still reading my letters? Without tapping away on your phone at the same time? Without compulsively changing the channel or the subject? Super. I felt it'd be better to write to you than speak to you. Your subordinates agreed.

Let's stop here for today. I don't want to waste my last few days of vacation.

Béatrice

MARCH 5,

MY DARLING,

I fear I'm the only one to love a tan so dark it would make you jealous. Yes, I'm well-rested, invigorated, and tan. Exactly what I needed.

I saw Clara, she sends her love. It was a quick visit, and we only spoke briefly—I wasn't going to spoil her birthday pouring out my soul and telling her how I've decided to change my life. A gaggle of friends and a cake (thirty candles) pair poorly with emotional cleanses. I don't know if she told you, but she felt bad that you didn't acknowledge it. I didn't dare bring up the previous years' birthdays and your recurrent bouts of amnesia.

How are you managing? Don't forget to pay Madame Grellier.

Béatrice

P.S.: I came by to take a few things and took the opportunity to water the plants.

MARCH 7,

GAËTAN,

("My Darling" was getting ridiculous)

One aspect of my letter-writing strategy will now change. But not the rules of the game—that would be too simple, or premature in any case. From this point forward, there will be no more envelopes on your desk. All my letters will now go to the house. Your house. (Because there will be other letters too...enough for a TV series).

I'll be mixing up the private with the professional. And we might quite unexpectedly meet again in the professional sphere.

Clara has still not received any birthday wishes from you; it's bordering on uncouth.

As for me, I've been learning more and more about you, and I know you're interested in what I have to say about that. Perhaps a little scared. Are you loosening up your tie, awkwardly unbuttoning your shirt collar?

I've witnessed that crude side of yours, which some of the men working under you seem to know all too well. Note how I'm intentionally abandoning the term "associate." Because no one works *with* you. *You* make the decisions, following orders of course, or more precisely following the national secretary's orders. But you're the one who takes action, who controls everything

—you alone. The others merely carry out your mandates. It's easy to get yourself off the hook by saying the orders came from above. Those kinds of "it's not me" scenarios have served to enable the worst events of History with a capital H. The events of our shared history too. It was all too easy to argue the group was to blame.

But I digress. Let's get back to our professional activities, since I remind you that I do have a life and a job. In an area quite removed from your own and, true, less prestigious, maybe even unimportant. But it's one that's been equally affected by the current fervor to destroy people's knowledge and run roughshod over them. So I finally came to a decision. I joined that dastardly band of trade unionists.

Uh-oh, I said it. That word you loathe. That you find passé. You want partners, associates, underlings eating out of your hand, suits waiting for you in low-lit offices. Not people who feel a little out of place in the halls of courthouses, but right at home out in the street, stereos in hand and flags held high. I admire those men and women for their dignity, their sense of community and justice. You could hardly imagine the energy required to fight for and defend a colleague when you yourself have been trampled, scorned, mistreated. I don't know how these people drum up the courage. I've always been terribly lacking in that department. As for you...

• • •

To be continued, without fail.

Béatrice

MARCH 9,

GAËTAN,

Me again. I bumped into Virginie. You know Virginie, your ex, the one before me. And also my old friend. We happened to cross paths a few months ago, and since then we've been meeting more and more. We've talked. About the good old days, and the not so good ones. And about you too, of course; rest assured. But something tells me you won't find that quite so reassuring.

We talked about you, about the others, our group of friends back then. About the late-night parties—and how you behaved. We would make up excuses for you, even though ultimately, they were for us. Excuses that shut us away in our denial (comfortably, we thought at the time).

As we spoke, stirring up the past, reflecting on it, we reached an agreement. And this won't set your mind at ease either. Am I wrong? Why not grab a drink so you can loosen up?

We'll talk again very soon. See you then—on paper.

Béatrice

MARCH 13,

NOTHING FRIENDLY THIS TIME. No opening, no first name. Straight to the point. Stop reading immediately if you can't take the fact that I *too* can get angry. You're not the only one who can flood a space with anger. Stop right now, but at the risk of it all remaining vague, unknown even. That little voice inside you will continually wonder: "what *else* was she able to dig up?" You'll go round and round in circles. You'll think of nothing else but never admit it to yourself. You'll fly off the handle (*"God, her letters annoy the shit out of me!"*). In a rage, you'll crumple up this sheet of paper and hurl it into the trash. You won't be able to sleep at night. But in the end you'll get up. You'll rifle through the bin, unfold the dirty piece of paper, and read it. What a waste of time and energy, don't you think?

So, yes, I'm angry, and therefore acting a bit coarsely. No big deal. I get annoyed when I think about your pitiful arguments defending yourself. That you weren't alone, that you were all involved. Yes, I am going back to that. Head-on. No, I didn't make a fresh start. Because you offered me nothing. This life, this comfort, our social status? I paid for them all, and dearly. Me alone. I don't give a damn about your money. I have my own.

Béatrice

MARCH 26,

WHAT'S your stance on free will? There's no disputing you work like a fiend, but isn't that your preference? To be a puppet held by the clawed hands of power? You think you're important, Monsieur Gaëtan Leroy "*with a y*," respected. Look at you, you're a marionette, a good little soldier. They use you. What did you learn at your elite schools about service and tractability, apart from how to feed off capitalism at others' expense? Bravo, you were such a good student. Honor roll for you! Obedience, and execution—that word rings so true for you. Congratulations! Do you scold a baker for making bread? No, of course not. Same for you and your cronies. You apply what you've learned, meticulously and submissively. Eyes closed. So go on then, why not show a little enthusiasm to boot? Is it out of ambition or to silence your conscience?

Béatrice

APRIL 3,

AND SO WE BEGIN AGAIN. Although a bit more calmly, in any case. Because we need to clear the ground Gaëtan, dig together through the wreckage of thirty-two years of living together, and move forward.

Let's go back to the beginning, to your work. Let's revisit your sacrosanct responsibilities, the veil you hide behind to avoid confrontation and dodge the truth. I'll be frank (cards on the table); I did some digging. Because an accusation requires precision and sound arguments. I had to know more about that time in your life that partially escapes me. I stumbled upon something, and it was way beyond what I'd hoped.

Despite the meager interest you have in my professional life, you know my job is at risk. That a deal's on the table for a major group to take over the company. Efficiency, agility, pooling resources, savings (or pseudo-savings). These are words that resonate just as much with you as "pressure" and "harassment" do in your management of your pawns.

Oh excuse me, I meant to say employees, salaried employees, who you hope will then voluntarily leave the playing field. It's easier, less expensive, and avoids conflict. You'll lick your lips and dash off to the next thing. It'll be win-win. Except when one of the two "winners" ends up at the bottom of a hole. Then it will just be collateral damage, predicted and planned, part and parcel in your world, where cynicism is the driving force. Sorry to point that out; please don't get all in a tizzy.

Standing not far from that hole, but at a distance where it was still permissible to react, was...me. Yes, me, Béatrice, your wife. Master's degree, executive in the fashion sector. Oh yes, fashion! Super women, great clothes. Hey, you should check the tags on your suits before you keep reading. Other colleagues were standing quite close to that hole. It swallowed up energy, hopes, and sometimes people's lives. They were in the so-called orange zone, where a person can still be found, and can still leave (beyond that, it's nothing but red). So right, the orange zone, all of the union people.

When you say "union," it's as if you were talking about furniture or concrete blocks. But these are *people,* Gaëtan. People, human beings. These are men and women who are sometimes a stone's throw away from the red zone, or even right on its edge. They're all in the same muck, but they have the will and the weapons to climb out of it. Weapons. Now that's a scary word isn't it?

And where does this violence come from? Well, there are administrative, legal, judicial, and human weapons. And most important of all, the power of a group. These are the people who pulled me back from the edge of the red zone.

It was not the three weeks of so-called rest, or the meds, or any of the other stuff I swallowed several times a day, paired with a big glass of your contempt.

Béatrice

APRIL 6,

I'LL GO AHEAD and continue, since I have a feeling you're going to find this extremely interesting. We were talking about getting the union involved, about defending people's rights, and saving their skin. With each meeting, I found myself further entrenched in this battle. To the point that when I attended a lunch at the national headquarters last fall, and some tables needed to be combined or separated (I can hardly remember which now), I ended up meeting some people from your company. They were quite chatty, and I know so much more about you now.

Take a deep breath, and sit back and relax. I didn't spill the beans or give my last name. In any case, it's not exactly unusual—we know several "Leroys" in our neighborhood alone. Plus, to all but a small group of people, I was just Béatrice at that point. Although by now they may very well have caught wind that I'm your wife, because of certain duties I've taken on very recently. Do go easy on the Scotch in any case.

One more little thing, before I sign off. The more I learn, the more I know you'll keep reading what I write. Because my letters are about your favorite subject—namely "you." Incidentally, I wonder if perhaps you're starting to get scared stiff.

I'll say it again—and know this is in your best interest: don't call in a union representative to ask about finding your wife.

Talk to you very soon.

Béatrice

APRIL 15,

GAËTAN,

Surprise! A card, to change things up a bit. It's an adorable Easter bunny, although I did not go and hide any eggs in the garden. Speaking of which, you're in charge of the roses; that goes without saying.

Do you remember Clara and her little baskets filled with chocolate eggs? Clara, so cute and smiley, so nicely dressed, with her hair all done up. A tiny model doll in the little home movies you'd so proudly show your friends. Friends who (in my opinion) couldn't have cared less. Where'd the time go? Can you believe how grown-up Clara is?

You *too* have aged, Gaëtan.

Béatrice

APRIL 20,

GAËTAN,

I hope you're not losing sleep over all this (this letter, the house to take care of, and my absence). Speaking of which, how *have* you been spending your nights? Per the rules of this epistolary game, it's a question that requires no answer. I'm simply curious. Perhaps you've already replaced me, although it's not likely. That would be too quick, plus it's not exactly a woman you need. More like a mistress of the house. Furthermore, I have a hard time imagining you in the arms of a lover.

In case you've been worrying about it, even as a matter of self-esteem, I didn't leave you *for* anyone else. I left *you*. I left the hypocrisy of what we'd become as a couple behind me, behind us. I left you to feel good in my own skin, the opposite of how it was in our two parallel lives. I left you with my eyes open. I left you to be free. Free to make peace with a past that I wanted to bury and that was sneakily eating away at me. The quicksand on which we built our life together caught up to us Gaëtan. There's nothing surprising about that.

I left you, but rest assured, I'm not going to leave you hanging, not anytime soon. However unpleasant my letters might sometimes be, I know they will become indispensable to you. A downright addiction. Very annoying, I agree. I know I'll be able to count on you being a loyal reader—it would be way too risky for you not to be.

I'm certain you're reading these letters at night, so I'll take the liberty of making a suggestion: take notes in the wee hours. Because nightmares tell us a lot about ourselves. Who knows, they might turn out to be very useful.

Béatrice

APRIL 25,

GAËTAN,

I'll get straight to the point. I miss you. It's idiotic, paradoxical, ridiculous, call it what you will, but it's true, I do miss you. We agree that the facts are clear—I'm the one who left, who abandoned the marital home. And with no prior notice. I'm the one at fault. You can rejoice, take advantage of it. It's pretty easy for me to imagine that were it reversed, you wouldn't miss me. You'd dive back into your newspaper, continuing to drone on about the results of the game. Which have nothing to do with you whatsoever, except for providing you with the illusion of a world that is no longer yours. Turn the TV back on. There's no danger to fear from this missive. You have the upper hand, you're in control. Better yet, you should feel flattered. What a treat! Top shelf! That's what my grandmother would have said.

If ever you resume reading later tonight, before collapsing from fatigue, or another day (what does it matter), take note of this: I miss your bad manners, your abruptness, your tactlessness. Your constant agitation about your precious self, your jokes, your bellowing laugh—your eyes that don't only undress *me*. On that topic, some of your colleagues don't love that your eyes tend to wander lower than theirs, nor are they thrilled by your angry outbursts. But me, I miss it all like a bad drug. Consider me to be in (voluntary) treatment. In detox. Finally.

Béatrice

MAY 6,

MUSIC, Gaëtan, music. I live in song and poetry.

Maybe I need the words of Serge Gainsbourg or Verlaine
to tell you I'm leaving.
Maybe I need to picture myself
on a train platform with Jean-Louis Aubert.
Perhaps I need to hear Boris Vian singing to me about the dead years,
about going on my way.
Or maybe it was Anne Sylvestre's voice
that allowed me to pack up and go.

Probably.

If you only knew how I delight in those "corny French songs" you loathed.

Béatrice

MAY 15,

GAËTAN,

My last two letters talked way too much about me and not enough about you: both for my taste and yours. So let's get back to discussing your practices, your professional practices. Is that better than bringing up old private, intimate memories? Should I spread this paper with all the filth accumulated under your clunky old man shoes, instead of the muck stuck to your CEO monkey suit? I don't know how I'd answer in your place. No one would want to be in your place.

In a previous letter, I alluded to your crude, chauvinistic behavior towards the women working under you. How in the middle of a meeting, your lustful eyes would shamelessly linger on more or less everything, your mind getting lost in fantasies light years away from the actual conversations. How you'd make people repeat things, get annoyed, not answer the questions asked. It's all as shocking as it is scornful. As I told you, I've met several of your female colleagues, who feel ridiculed and wounded that you neither listen to nor hear them, just because they're women. They were more than happy to talk about your behavior, your contempt, your vulgarity.

They talked about how aggressive you are. They can't take any more of your critiques about their bodies or your obscene banter. Nor are they willing to keep feeling you undress them with your libidinous looks. You've really stooped low, Gaëtan.

Men, too, (happily) are complaining about your blatant machismo. I was not surprised to hear that they too blame you for using discrimination as a management method. Have you really not even a shred of honesty?

As for your dealings with your friends' wives, you know as well as I do that some of them could attest to such behavior. Definitely an avenue to explore.

Stay tuned...

Béatrice

MAY 23,

GAËTAN,

The tragic thing about contempt and cynicism is that the facts (and therefore the evidence) are minimized in favor of feelings and impressions. When you talk about restructurings, pooling of resources, profitability, race for profit, when you say cash, wealth, efficiency (that magic word; here, I'll write it again, *efficiency*), I hear contempt, suffering, loss of self-confidence, denial of individuals, mourning a part of one's life. I see pawns on a massive gameboard, and above all, I hear you laughing. But I'm not playing anymore Gaëtan. It's over. I've changed sides and I'm going to fight you. You in particular, but your accomplices too. I needed to be unencumbered, so I went away. Not only from you—that was already true, and it was mutual. But also away from our marital home. It's done now. We'll talk about it again, our marriage, our shared past. It's in process. But I'm not playing anymore. Furthermore, this new freedom is opening doors for me. And I think it's game over for you.

Béatrice

JUNE 1,

GAËTAN,

Let's maintain this little ritual of ours. These one-way letters that I continue to write to you. I neither need nor want any replies. Thirty-two years of life together have enabled me to guess them, sometimes even foresee them. Oh Gaëtan, you're so predictable! Imagine for a moment that this correspondence stopped, that the mailbox turned up empty, desperately empty. First you'd be relieved, but it would be short-lived. Then you'd feel the void. You'd compulsively open and close the mailbox, perhaps several times in a row. To check, to make sure. Still empty? Then each of the following nights, nothing, not even Saturday morning. First you'd feel the void. Then, as the anguish gradually set in, you'd start wondering: *"What else could she have up her sleeve?"*

You've become familiar with my letter-writing process. And don't worry, I'm not done yet. Especially because my conversations with Virginie have increased. Conversations about the past, one of our favorite subjects. Just picture us, two old girlfriends. People used to say we were inseparable back then. And we were—until you came into the picture. It was a classic series of events: flirtation, betrayal, a falling out, leaving. Silence.

Virginie moved back to the area last year. At first we'd just exchange pleasantries here and there, but by now we have grown quite close. I know how impatient you are. Virginie is equally so, and she's burning to see you again. And not necessarily so she can throw herself into your arms.

We'll keep you informed. A meeting after such a long time requires planning.

Béa

How long has it been since you called me that little nickname, "Béa"? Virginie just plucked it out from her memory.

JUNE 3,

THE NEXT INSTALLMENT, as promised. You'd find it amusing to see the two of us, Virginie and me, once again the best of friends. *Once again.* You can glimpse a whole complicated past from those two words. But now it's time to move on. We've taken matters into our own hands—Virginie especially. We've found one another again. There are still beautiful gifts in this life. The past is the past. And yet, Gaëtan. And yet...

Know that we have reached an agreement. We've come to a decision. Virginie will also be writing to you (sorry to spoil the surprise). Perhaps not as regularly as me. But you'll not be wanting for reading material! I wonder if some of your colleagues have started to make any written records of events or remarks. This writing fever is spreading, and all thanks to you, our hero.

See you on paper, so soon.

Béa or Béatrice?

I forgot, just one piece of advice for you, since you care so much about your appearance. Ask Madame Grellier to come more often. That way she'll be able to iron several shirts for you in advance.

JUNE 6,

GAËTAN,

A truce, a compromise, a pact. A surrender? Don't count on it. Call it what you want, but here's what I'm proposing. Let's meet on the 24th of this month in the Verdon Forest. I'm letting you know in advance so you can plan accordingly. I'll handle everything—music, razzle-dazzle, decorating the space for dancing, good ambiance, and drinks. Cocktail attire please!

Some of my friends will be joining us. That's my only condition and I will not compromise on this point. There will be several of us. You'll be alone, and the party will continue until we're exhausted and can't go on. Until we can't play another song, take another bite, take any more of you, that's for sure. The Milky Way will dance above our heads. The moon (I'm counting on it!), the trees, and even the hills will spin—the whole forest will become a dance hall. By daybreak you'll be groggy, punch-drunk, and so happy to have seen me again.

I'm proposing this crazy night to you Gaëtan, which you'll remember for the rest of your life. Don't let this chance pass you by; there won't be any others.

Rest assured, I'll provide you with more details very soon.

Looking forward to it.

Béatrice

JUNE 12,

GAËTAN,

Thirty-two years. Approximately eleven thousand six hundred days. Of finding excuses for you, of piecing together a suit that's too big and too beautiful for you. I saw you as a dashing young man—beautiful blue eyes, athletic (at the time), seductive, funny, a joker whether we were alone or in the company of your friends. Those inseparable friends who we never distrusted enough. That feeling of partying to excess, sometimes (oh rarely, very rarely), to the point of crossing the line. Was it once, just the once? Extenuating circumstances, we could say.

We looked like a pretty little family, the ideal couple. Clara came along very quickly, and she was so cute. We were model parents at all the school meetings and fairs, the weekend sports events and dinners with grandparents. You still hung out with the guys, except they had girlfriends now. Clara would leap onto their tender knees. Clara, who loves life, who looks so much like you. She has the same eyes, the same style. We were the perfect family, we looked like an ad.

You still hold your place as father, no issue there. But the time will come that you'll have to answer for yourself. It will take time, a lot of time, given that you've been covering your tracks. Acting too perfectly. Too everything.

I've held on, Gaëtan, these thirty-two years. I've waited for the appropriate moments, imagined, plotted, devised a plan, of which these letters are just one visible part. Patience, patience. You'd never be able to show a steadfastness equal to the one I've lived with for these past three decades. But waiting one's turn can have its advantage. I repainted our life together in the colors that suited me. It was a vital process, for Clara, and for me.

You must be aware that it's become hard for me to see our life through rose-colored glasses these past few years. In a way, since our daughter, *our* daughter, became an adult. I'm daring to hope that you would not go so far as to make her, even subconsciously, feel responsible for your distance. Once Clara left, you began to change, then more and more, to the point that I have a hard time recognizing you now. Or is it me that has finally managed to open her eyes?

I'll let you mull my last question over.

Béatrice

JUNE 17,

GAËTAN,

People could blame me for being so blind, for staying all those years. They could accuse me of hypocrisy, Machiavellianism, maybe even mental impairment—*how could she both bury her head in the sand* and *plot her revenge?* I couldn't argue with that. I was one of the imbeciles and simpletons to defend you. But we'd need to call Virginie to the stand (going even further back) and hear her attest to the years of flirtation with you. We'd need to talk about your activities at that time, with all your bros and your so-called joy rides. That would be a fitting moment to hear her side of things as well.

The accusations against me would then start to pale in comparison. Because others would be called to the stand too. Victims of that people-wrecking machine—a system that only works because some men and women agree to work within it. You know who I'm thinking of. But they were also victims of a man's schemes. Victims of you, Gaëtan Leroy, the perfect manager. These witnesses will not paint a very flattering portrait of you. They'll strip away the image of you as the perfect father, the perfect friend. And when a boat gets too flimsy, it sinks.

. . .

Prepare your defense, Gaëtan. Otherwise, even the imbeciles and morons in the courtroom will start to have some serious doubts.

Béatrice

JUNE 20,

TRULY, everyone is writing to you, Gaëtan! My letters are all the rage. Seriously though, you should have received a letter. From the national secretary's office. News of this matter is starting to get around. It's a letter reminding you of the law. Because it's true, even a corporate bigwig like yourself can't know every single clause. But you should be made aware of the limits. I fear your position and status as director will only make all this worse. And you should have anticipated the legitimate anger of your victims.

I don't doubt you'll have explanations to give the supervising officer, inventive treasures deployed to convince him of your good faith. You'll invoke that ordinary, banal, stock-in-trade sexism you've used elsewhere, even though attacking others makes for a poor defense. And I'm even more confident that you'll try (for a time) to change your behavior and your remarks.

I'm way more skeptical about your ability to endure a summons at the administrative court.

Béatrice

JUNE 23,

GAËTAN,

Would I alone have the courage needed to confront all those people who would look the other way and take your side...the side of a compulsive liar...*Thirty some-odd years later...and all this time she stayed with him*...It'd be my word against theirs. Well I would, yes, but there's also Virginie. It happened to her the year before it happened to me. Virginie, who no one would listen to at the time, and who did not stay with you. *She had some nerve, that brazen lady. What is that stupid woman talking about? It was nothing serious, just one entry in the log book, quickly filed away as soon as she left the police station.*

But the vise is tightening, Gaëtan, because there are two of us now. It's Virginie and Béatrice, we're decided on that. Two women, supported by their friends. Two women, plus justice. Plus a certain young man named Loïc. Do you remember Loïc? He's a little older than Clara? Virginie must have mentioned him in her letters. Incidentally, Virginie often confides in Loïc. He's a tormented boy who is not very fond of you.

And Clara? With Clara, our daughter, it's a bit different. She adored you—well, until now. Oh yes, Gaëtan, Clara knows. Everything. I had wanted to save her from the sordid parts, but would that have actually been a good idea...would I have been doing her a favor...? Clara is a terrific girl who supports me and understands me. Now she knows and it's a relief. It makes a big difference, doesn't it? Time, courage, and my determination will help her move beyond the shock.

Tomorrow. We'll go tomorrow, Virginie and I. Then we'll celebrate in your company. Reassure me, would you, that you haven't forgotten? Verdon Forest, 10 p.m., Route de la Morte Bouteille, that goes without saying—put on your GPS for once, you get lost so easily—and dress well.

See you tomorrow,

Béatrice

J-L

part two

CLARA

"THIS IS *the National Police Force. I'd like to speak with Clara Leroy, please."*

How could anyone sleep after a telephone call as brutal as that? Despite the efforts and tact of the person on the other end of the line, the words fell on Clara like a string of successive, unconnected detonations. *Accident, father, speed, forest road, tree, I'm sorry, all of a sudden, nothing could be done.* A puzzle of an accident that her brain took several seconds to piece together and finally realize what they were telling her—that her father was dead. A phone that rang at a time that was already in and of itself worrisome. An unknown number, the police. And then she, like a robot, putting her clothes back on to go out, going to the hospital, giving her name at the front desk, traversing deserted hallways, finding herself in an icy basement, then returning to her house, her head in a fog.

And the now-indelible image of her father's face. Was it a nightmare, some farfetched scenario? Maybe it was her imagination. Maybe the night and her fatigue were playing tricks on her. Yet there were the words, inserted into the official document she'd carried back in her handbag "...declares the death...Gaëtan Leroy... June 24..."

At least she can be sure of it now. Before she calls her mother...well it's already tomorrow morning. She'll need to go to the house. After all, she has the keys, and it's not so far. They asked her to bring in her father's personal effects—clothing, papers. She'd written everything down. The list is indeed there, right in front of her. Sad and confirmed. Clara gets back in the car (no matter that it's the middle of the night) and goes to his house, their house. It's messy now with her mother gone, but it's still their house, her parents' house.

If the reality were not so brutal and destabilizing, unlocking the front door to her old house in the dark of night might remind her of many a trip home from a nightclub. She moves deeper into the living room, chasing away the fleeting images. She tiptoes in like a thief, like a child cracking open the door to her parents' bedroom. Enough. This is ridiculous. She turns on the light.

She's an adult. She has to figure things out, confront the situation, and bring back what they've asked. She'll call her mother, of course. Tomorrow morning. Will she talk about these diaries and photos scattered more or less everywhere, the cushions on the floor, that bottle of whiskey? He'd certainly made some headway on the bottle, but then she'd have been surprised to find otherwise. No glass. That was new. So he was taking swigs before he went and smashed himself against a tree and abandoned us. Clara is flustered. Sad, beaten, but also agitated, angry almost. At her father and at the whole world.

A hunch leads her to the kitchen garbage can and

recycling bin. There are no more bottles, she can hear the emptiness. She'll go and check the cellar. Clara returns to the living room, nervously pushing aside copies of *l'Équipe* newspapers. She discovers a package of envelopes and letters all mixed together, turning white as she recognizes her mother's handwriting. She suddenly hates herself for rummaging around like this. Who does she think she is? She collapses onto the sofa, letting her pain and tears erupt. All the pressure of these last several hours lands. She's cold and alone, smack dab in the center of the living room. The living room of her absent, deserter parents.

Why? How?

Her mother's departure had come first, followed by the explosion of her revelations. They hadn't had time to talk about it again. Clara is still in shock. And now a deadly accident, and this packet of letters. Her shivering grows stronger. She grabs a quilt, wipes away her tears, and nods off. A few moments, a few hours.

She glances at the clock. She had indeed fallen asleep.

CLARA AND BÉATRICE

HER PHONE CONVERSATION with Béatrice was fast, too fast. Overcome by her pain, Clara could only utter a few words, and right away her mother understood that they were fatal. Although completely confused by her feelings, Béatrice knew she urgently needed to go and join Clara. It was strange to come back to this house which used to be (actually still is) hers, the one where she lived as a married woman. Her household. Should the fact that she'd left a few months ago prevent her from mourning?

A car ride later and here they are reunited, seesawing between emotions, embraces, outpourings. Clara will try to put on a good show for a few more hours, despite the fire that's been growing inside of her since reading the letters early this morning. By the end, the stinging words and burning sentences had left her in complete shock. She was as much stunned by the tone and vehemence of the words as she was impressed by her mother's boldness.

For the time being, she would inform family, friends and professional contacts, get the house and papers in order, then give the two of them some space from the emotional pandemonium. But only for a time.

Béatrice is not the best situated to organize the

funeral arrangements. Many people know the couple had separated. But she still has to play the wife—if nothing else, for Clara's sake. Béatrice is swimming in ambiguity. She can't just let her daughter manage everything, yet she dreams of being far from here, far from this charade. But not now, not yet. Not before she's gone to Gaëtan's funeral, not before she again hears the women he worked with accuse him, not before she's clarified certain things with Virginie.

And she must think about Clara, Clara above all. So many questions are lurking beneath the surface, between mother and daughter.

JUNE 25TH IN THE VERDON GAZETTE

Accident in Verdon Forest Saturday Night: CEO of France-ADM Killed on Contact

A DEADLY ACCIDENT OCCURRED YESTERDAY, *Friday, June 24th, in the early evening in the Verdon Forest, Route de la Morte Bouteille. The driver (the sole passenger in the vehicle) died after violently crashing into a tree on the roadside. A motorcyclist apparently called an ambulance. When the paramedics arrived on the scene, there was nothing more they could do.*

The weather was mild, and the road was completely dry. From the initial evidence, the investigation concluded that the driver, who was clearly quite intoxicated, had lost control of the vehicle. Although this forest road gets very little traffic, the police are nonetheless launching a call for witnesses to find anyone who might have seen the tragic accident occur.

BÉATRICE

BÉATRICE HESITATED about where to live for the few days (or more) of formalities following the death. Then she got in her car and drove from her new residence to her old house. Turning down Clara's offer to stay with her, Béatrice had ultimately chosen her old home, which was in a neighborhood close to Clara's. She placed her hastily packed weekend bag in the guest room. No way would she share the marital bed with a ghost. Beyond being quite rightfully upset, Clara seemed tense, nervous, and even hostile towards Béatrice. Yet when Béatrice had finally opened up to her a few days ago, her daughter nonetheless promised her full support.

Yet Gaëtan's death had changed the landscape. And Clara had no doubt found (and read) the letters, as she was the first to arrive on the night of his death. Only that could explain her daughter's distant attitude. Clara would need time to digest, understand, and overcome all these hardships, but Béatrice was hopeful they'd eventually be as close as before. If the letters were not sufficiently clear, she'd explain. She'd take the time to discuss the whys and hows. But how many months, how many years would it take to have a complete, sincere, and dispassionate discussion?

CLARA

A NIGHT SONG dances in Clara's mind. Images endlessly superimposed one over the next. Her mind's an increasingly tortured tangle where one memory becomes embedded in a photo, another in a letter. Again and again. The later it gets, the more the resulting images resemble those little squares they used to color in different shades to make one final drawing. Yet now the result is distorted by the rhythm of the coloring, worsening in this night without end.

She sees her father's knees, his arms, his laugh; after-school snacks, vacations. The terrible vitriolic words on paper, the despicable words of truth, the intolerable image of a young woman held against a tree by three men. The face of that young woman, the features of her mother deformed, a car smashed against a tree. Was it the same tree? Who were those men? More snapshots follow of family meals, joyful Sundays, photos of the three of them, her parents and her.

She then sees her mother's words again, those letters, those accusations, accusations from colleagues too. And that mess she found in the empty living room, which her mother had fled in January, her father in June. Everyone jumping ship—what have they been playing at? Clara is alone. The love has vanished too, if there ever was any in this family. Did love ever fill this home?

And were all those images fake? Had she invented her

childhood, her happiness? Had she invented her parents, or the icy hallways of the hospital she'd rushed to yesterday after that late-night phone call?

Who is lying to whom? Where is the truth in her own life? What was her mother's truth? Who colored those tiny squares that were now spinning faster and faster in her head? Who was her father and towards what death did he plunge that June night?

LOÏC

LOÏC STANDS at the back of the crematorium. After hesitating for quite a while, he'd finally decided to come to the funeral. But sitting down would mean agreeing to participate in what he would later call a farce. He'd warned them. He would be there, but nothing more than that. He should not be asked to go along with any sham ceremony, or carry a coffin, or be given flowers to place on top of it, let alone make a speech or engage in any tearful embraces. In any case, he does not know, as it were, the deceased. He's calling him "the deceased" for the time being. Later he'll decide whether or not he can call him "Gaëtan." And actually, Loïc is not displeased about his privileged position as witness, son, or friend. Someone whose presence is expected (or perhaps dreaded?).

Plus, from this end of the room, just alongside the exit, he can observe. For example, the people who compulsively look at their watches, their palms returning to their cellphones, and others (not knowing how to whisper) who exchange little text messages with one another. *"For the next funeral, we should plan to have a livestream on everyone's smartphones,"* he thinks, surprising himself.

Only Clara's tears seem to be sincere. And yet. What father is she crying for? The one from a happy childhood? The one from recent years, who as far as Loïc knew, was nasty and arrogant? How is she mourning this bastard of a parent? Another mystery he'll stay away from, his eyes dry.

Béatrice is truly uncomfortable, feigning sadness, embarrassed by her pain, which has shown up like an impostor. Then there's Virginie. Haughty, cold, out of place. The discomfort is palpable. As for the others, everyone else...He figures some of them are Clara's friends, some the deceased's so-called buddies. No doubt missing (or at least maybe) are his two old sidekicks from the Verdon Forest. They'd have cut all ties with the deceased long ago. And if they hadn't, they wouldn't have dared shown their faces here. But he'll check, he'll ask around. Then there's that group of guys over there, sitting shamelessly in the first few rows; the full staff of the grieving administration. All that's missing is the national secretary himself.

Were all these people here to mourn the hero of the hour, or to see him disappear forever? As far as he's concerned, he knows the answer. And he'll do everything he can to get an answer out of Béatrice. He needs to understand. What's the point of this grotesque gathering? Why are they here, Béatrice, Virginie, and even Clara, their faces painted in sorrow? Who are they seeing off to the afterlife?

These obsessive questions are futile distractions. He'd allowed his mind to wander. Yet now Loïc has suddenly returned to this ominous room, with its false sadness, artificial decor, and duplicitous warmth. Everything seems fake. Who do these men in black think they are, presiding over everything—priests? Masters of a broken family they'll forget a few minutes later? Everyone gets up, many of them head towards the exit, some of them nearly shoving him to get to the condolence book. There was a terrible car accident. A CEO, such a great man. What an immense loss. So much pain. So much compassion.

Tiny groups of people form outside, around Béatrice, around Clara, or both of them together, or around Virginie, joined a short time after by Loïc. "Do you know my son? He recently moved back to the area too. A few months ago." Blah blah blah. He has no desire to delve into these empty conversations, nor to hear how they knew him when he was little and how much he's grown, or that he looks so much like his mother. But no one dares mention his father. More than thirty years earlier, their tongues were certainly freer, searing into Virginie with all kinds of scathing descriptors. Strange how a father is accused less of being a bastard than the mother of being a slut. Or worse, Loïc thinks, discreetly moving away. He gives a tiny polite wave to Béatrice along the way, who is deep in conversation with the deceased's officers and professional coterie. How does she do it? This ceremony, painted in the colors of hypocrisy and false pretense, is decidedly grotesque. To avoid stirring up this hornet's nest, Loïc chooses to leave. He's respected his commitments. He came and watched his step, and there was no drama. Better to slip away now.

CLARA

CLARA DOES NOT BELIEVE it was just a normal car accident. Not her father, not all alone, in the middle of the forest. Speed, definitely, alcohol, fine. She's had no choice but to accept the results of the blood analysis that was done immediately after discovering the tragedy. She knows her father. And everyone has their guilty pleasure or strategy of avoidance when the pressure gets to be too much. He was indulged in that respect. Being a CEO is not stress-free, and she'd understood that he had difficult decisions weighing on him, although he'd said very little to her about them.

One question, that she's trying very hard to push away, nevertheless haunts her: what if, *despite everything,* her mother had gone too far?

For days, Clara has been repeating that word, *rape*, on loop. It's like a shockwave has just stricken her, crashing full-force into her memories of being a little girl adored by a loving father. Her mother had had oh so many reasons to talk to her about it. Clara had of course supported her mother's plan to file a joint complaint with Virginie. But what was she, Gaëtan's daughter, supposed to do with all these discoveries and revelations? And what should she think about all those letters? The whole thing was strange. She'd found those letters a bit too easily. As if her father had wanted (planned?) for other readers to intrude into the living room, or just her,

Clara, for whom he would have largely facilitated the task. Did he sense that all this might end badly? Did he *want it to*? Clara has been trying to push away this troublesome scenario since that night in June, overwhelmed by a terrible feeling of ambivalence.

Nonetheless, she can't quite believe the accident theory. The road is relatively straight at the spot where the car hit the tree. And her father was an excellent driver. Sure, he was a little drunk, but Clara had (unfortunately) had occasion to note that it did not impact his driving.

As the days continued to pass, more and more doubt emerged alongside her sorrow, her support for her mother, and her attempts to understand a father who'd eluded her. And that's not even considering that Loïc boy, who was now suddenly and mysteriously back in the spotlight.

BÉATRICE AND VIRGINIE

VIRGINIE WAITED until after the funeral. After all the formalities, and Clara and Béatrice's summonses before the police. She waited for the right moment, when their respective children were not there, and no one else was either. But she would not let Béatrice slip away—they needed to talk.

This afternoon, the two of them are finally alone, at Virginie's house. The hardest days are behind them. The investigation into the accident now appears to have been closed. This evening could, *should*, look like drinks between friends. A mix of relaxation and confidences, that delicate alchemy of which friendship is the secret ingredient. They've managed to have it these past few months. Light little reprieves that allowed hearts to open, a bit of balm placed over difficult words.

But tonight Virginie is tense. It's no doubt the result of having held back her impatience so long, combined with some degree of guilty conscience. Because after all, should she really be complaining? She'd lost neither a husband nor a father, just sleep. And perhaps a friend. She can't take this weight on her conscience anymore. The police, the filing of the complaint, facts that go back thirty years at the end of the day. And plus, doesn't life just go on?

But then Gaëtan randomly got himself killed behind the wheel that night. While under pressure, drunk, not to mention dealing with those harassing letters from Béatrice, and her own letters too. She'd allowed herself to be influenced, which is not like her. "What came over us, Béa? And the sleepless nights, the puffy eyes—don't lie to yourself, you're not sleeping either. What's to blame? Your so-called sorrow or your guilty conscience? Your leaving home last January, everything that's happened since, and everything you've dragged me into?"

Virginie is as angry at herself as she is at her friend. Although in her heart of hearts, she knows the only one who ever forced her into anything was Gaëtan. She went and filed a complaint of her own free will. But she can't admit it anymore. It's more reassuring to put all the responsibility on Béatrice. It's a tiny, insidious move that (she believes) will exonerate her a little.

Béatrice is not turning back. She knew Virginie as lucid, willing, determined, and independent. Tonight, she's found her to be caustic, unfair, and above all, amnesic. "How can you minimize these despicable facts? Did you forget, my dear, that you got raped? On the night of a party, by three bastards? Do you want me to refresh your memory with some vivid details? Honestly, can you look me straight in the eye and tell me you believe the statute of limitations should stand?

Me? I was naïve and blind. I believed it was a fleeting deviation. I believed the convoluted explanations and excuses. But not you, Virginie. You saw more clearly, you were braver. So don't go telling me nonsense now. It took me years to understand, to discover the real Gaëtan. A man who was perverted, twisted, and cynical, including in his professional life. But ultimately I agreed with you.

We didn't do anything wrong, Virginie. Let's not mistake the enemy here. Justice will do its work, and I do believe in justice. All we did was write down some facts and our perception of those facts. We wrote about what our lives have been like since what happened. It's never a crime to write the truth. The truth, Virginie. Get a good night's sleep and wake up with your eyes open!"

VIRGINIE AND LOÏC

THERE'S a palpable tension between Loïc and Virginie. He asks his mother to sit down, as he continues pacing the room. Virginie refuses to listen to him until he calms down. Virginie argues that she's tired and Loïc retorts that she wasn't too tired to put on airs at that bastard's funeral, or to spend the evening out with her girlfriend Béa, reliving "the good old days." Then the two of them get into a pretty heated discussion, quite the opposite of their usual rapport.

Loïc is still agitated. He doesn't want to calm down because being calm is the easy way out, and he can't take any more of it. He's stayed calm for—just how many years of calm has it been? Enough. Are you and Béatrice happy now? You've filed a complaint, you've done what you had to do, and now it's time to move on! Loïc continues, saying things about that asshole who crashed into a tree, all alone, that asshole Gaëtan who supposedly paid, that consequently, we could move on now.

So that's your theory then?

And now he's laying into Clara, who's lost her beloved daddy, what a pity, the poor thing. And Loïc who just won't let up...Goddamn it!

Virginie, who in the end took a seat, now stands back up. It's too much for her, and he shouldn't be speaking to her like this. They'll resume this sad excuse for a conversation later.

But Loïc's not done. He regrets having accompanied Virginie to that bastard's funeral. Yes, he still thinks he was a bastard, turning a deaf ear to his mother's protests right to the end. He tells her what he thinks. That she didn't need to be there, that neither of them did. Especially not her. Béatrice neither, nor Clara for that matter. Gaëtan should have left this world alone, with his pals and no one else.

You two are the queens of hypocrisy.

So then justice. Yes, he knows, justice with a capital J. But how many years did it take you before you went back to the police? And with Gaëtan dead, has justice *actually* been served?

So then, fine, Virginie would be happy to sit down and have a discussion, but Loïc must listen to her too. Virginie reminds him of what she did at the time, how she went to the police, how no one listened to her. She had already told him. She does not need to be schooled by him. She'd left with her little Loïc, so she could move far away from Gaëtan. She did what she could to put herself back together and raise him. So just stop. Please.

As for his reproaches of Béatrice, he should address them to her. Nothing is simple in life. Yes, Béatrice had stayed with Gaëtan, but she'd also made his life miserable these past few months.

Virginie goes on. Now that Loïc has stopped getting all worked up, she can talk about Gaëtan. She tells him, as she had already done, about their youth, their friends, the Saturday night parties. Béatrice was already part of the group. So were the guys who would binge drink, then go out on their "joy rides," as they used to call them. Her stories always circle back to that night that ended so badly. Loïc was little, his grandmother would often babysit him. She remembers that Béatrice wasn't there. Virginie had thought she was off having fun with the group, blowing off some steam. She'd come back forever wounded. She was battered, in every sense of the word, well beyond what anyone could imagine.

She herself had fled "like a thief," people said at that time. She was angry with everyone, but incapable of explaining herself after such a shock. She had lost everything, her work, her friends. But thanks to him, Loïc, her son, she had found the energy and courage to embark on another life, elsewhere. The two of them, alone. He knew about all that, she'd already told him, but he should understand that the circumstances were different now. And then, not holding back, she told him that while Loïc might only have lived here for a short time, he definitely knew Gaëtan's address, so if he'd had so many things to say to him, why hadn't he gone and spoken to him *directly*?

It was no doubt the straw that broke the camel's back. Now even more determined to get out of there, Loïc gave his reply, which Virginie in all likelihood did not hear, drowned as it was by the slam of the front door: "Maman, you have no idea."

BÉATRICE

THE UNION HEADQUARTERS are a change of scenery for Béatrice, who is attending the last meeting before the summer break. Although break does not mean truce. They've planned to take turns, or more literally, alternate patrols. There have been low blows during summer vacations. It's a very strange meeting for her, since she's hesitant about hanging back, even staying a bit on the defensive. It's ridiculous, because it's not about her today. It's about Gaëtan. The ties that brought them together are now out in the open, but what rock could they throw at her? Would being the wife of a bastard make her a suspect? A pariah? Practically everyone here knows and appreciates her commitment and the stances she's taken. Does she need to lay bare her private life to dispel suspicions? Exposing what she'd suffered would serve no purpose, or it could be worse—she'd need to forever be explaining herself, justifying herself—and this is not the place. In any case, news of the complaint she filed against Gaëtan is going to get around, even if it's judged to be null. There's no point mentioning it now.

Béatrice pulls herself together. She has nothing to feel ashamed of, quite the contrary. She's not a "wife of," she's not the "wife of the CEO of France-ADM." Even though he's dead. She's Béatrice, a national union representative. Still. Despite the report from a manager, some people still have their doubts. Traces of misogyny continue to throw a wrench in activism. It's the paradox of the battle against oppression; like Captain Haddock in *Tintin* and that band-aid that won't come off.

"First, a bit of gallows humor: we'll spare you the moment of silence. Where were we on the Administrative Court proceedings?" One colleague's meager attempt to lighten the already tense atmosphere. Followed by the report on the status of an investigation Béatrice knows well because she has tracked it from the start. Administrative terms, legal terms. Cold, impersonal, still at the paperwork phase—the registered letters, their replies. Béatrice listens less and less. She's lost in her thoughts and memories, her mind a tangle of blame, justification, and plans for the future. They almost seem to have forgotten she's here, and that's exactly what she wanted. For there to be no fuss or bother with her.

She's heard her name, part of a biting retort in the current conversation. "It's not because he didn't know how to drive—excuse us Béatrice." They must be talking about Gaëtan, about his death, which naturally deprived everyone of justice—her, Virginie, all these women. "It's fine, go ahead. Say what you have to say." Despite the concerted efforts Béatrice has made for weeks to look reality in the face, she cannot help but stiffen up. She knows how they've gotten here. She's all too familiar with the report of serious offenses. Testimonies from victims of that other Monsieur Leroy. It had been decided that the plaintiffs would tell their stories in their own words. The accounts were a bit awkward in some cases, but always very sincere.

"Walking into an office where two of us were, Monsieur Leroy called out, looking at us, 'is anyone else here? I'll come back then'; because his male colleague wasn't there."

"Right in the middle of the Planning Committee meeting, while I was presenting our findings on the asbestos matter to him, and this was in front of the engineering office's experts, he cut me off to say 'what a very pretty necklace you're wearing; it looks phenomenal on you' without listening to a word of my analysis."

"At another committee meeting, Monsieur Leroy blatantly turned and stared at a female colleague who had bent down to pick up her bag, since she had to leave early. As you may have guessed, this colleague was wearing a skirt."

"During an office visit with the female department head, he didn't look us in the eyes, but in the breasts, barely listening to us, or not listening at all." And so on.

The union president resumed speaking: "and then there are, in the confidential document, detailed personal testimonies; for example, from female coworkers who were called into his office and did not walk back out unscathed. They were pressured, he'd repeatedly make lewd allusions, leer, make rather inappropriate gestures, then put his hands where they shouldn't be as he walked them back out the door. Where there were no witnesses —how convenient."

Béatrice has heard these women speak in the most private, restricted meetings. They'd confided their most intimate details, which they would not be attesting to here, not today. Right down to the details that had to be inferred from their words. Béatrice senses and understands that these are wounds of the soul more than the body. For her, the question is still, and will always be: how could she *not* superimpose the many faces of Gaëtan onto these words, whether whispered, shouted, sometimes even wept?

She knows these women are courageous. They say the same about her. But is it courage to open her eyes to the true nature of a man with whom she shared so many years, her daughter's father? Isn't it more just a selfish necessity to allow her to go on?

CLARA

CLARA PREFERS TO be alone tonight. She's been having rough nights for two weeks now, the cumulative effect of fatigue, truths revealed, and too many emotions. Too much work—too much everything. She needs silence, rest, solitude. Her mother will understand. Clara is hoping for at least one night, just one little night, to distance herself from this absurd disconnect between the shadow of her father, now irremediably marred by the word bastard written in indelible ink, and the heap of paradoxical images of a happy little family with model parents. Especially from the images of her mother, inlaid in filigree into Clara's mind, along with the unrelenting question: how was this woman able to live with this man all those years?

She won't think about it, just for a few hours. She'll stop thinking about anyone or anything. Put her head in the sand. Sink into the quicksand of mindless television so she can forget this gloomy slew of questions. Stay deaf to the noise of the pounding hammer, like a rusted nail. To all those letters slammed into the warped head of a father she no longer recognizes, an accused who is no longer around to answer for his actions. She'll silence that little voice that insidiously whispered words of vengeance and manipulation beside her mother's signature. Just stick to the detailed accounts of Béatrice and Virginie, to their filed complaint. Follow the court's process. Not listen to anyone else. Most importantly, she won't give in to accusatory siren calls. She won't get the victim wrong.

She had hoped to be thinking about something else, at least tonight, and then go to sleep. But there's nothing for it, and these mysteries keep appearing on loop, like a litany. Why did her mother stay with her father during all of those years of silence, false pretenses, and lies? What exactly happened that gruesome June night, on a straight road in the middle of the Verdon Forest? How could her father have been so afraid that he lost all control? Had he decided to end things, refusing to face the mountain of private and professional accusations against him? Did her mother literally push him to his edge? Or, or...She finally dares to formulate it. Had someone "helped" him, meddled with his car, for example? She thinks hard...no, now she's just inventing. Yet how can you know? What do you do with all these doubts, poised to soon spin out of control?

What do you do aside from chase them away, push them back, trample them? Perhaps simply accept the theory of an accident, or fatality. Her father killed himself in a car. That's all there is. His death belongs to him. He is, whether directly or not, the main person responsible. Tonight she's taken her head out of the sand and opened her eyes, and decided to stop inventing scenarios and asking unanswerable questions. There's only one question she cares about, and that one she'll ask her mother.

JULY 7TH IN THE VERDON GAZETTE

Unexpected Developments Concerning the Death of the CEO of France-ADM,
Several Complaints Were Previously Filed.

A REMINDER OF THE FACTS: *This past June 24th, a deadly accident in the Verdon Forest (involving a single vehicle) killed Gaëtan Leroy, the driver and the only person in the car. The vehicle had violently crashed into an oak tree alongside the road; at the time, alcohol and speed were considered to be the clear causes of the tragedy.*

Should we see a connection between the two complaints filed the morning of the deadly accident, which directly targeted Gaëtan Leroy, although we have not been informed of the precise facts?

Our investigative department will update you as soon as we have shed light on this matter, which is starting to look more complex than a common car accident.

CLARA AND BÉATRICE

NEITHER ONE OF them hides from the moment. There's no standing on ceremony. Nothing that could prevent this discussion, which they know is inevitable. Clara and Béatrice are facing one another. They have each spontaneously sat down in an armchair. Neither one of them attempted the couch, which might have brought them closer, restored the tenderness and intimacy that the recent events had stolen from them. They no doubt prefer to look at one another. Face to face. They look at each other for a long time, intimidated. As if they weren't mother and daughter. There's no more music or songs. Which one of them will decide to break the silence? And where to start?

"Sweetie pie."

At the exact second she opens her mouth, Béatrice knows she's made a mistake.

"Sweetie pie" evokes Clara's happy, carefree youth. Their model family, a tight-knit trio—or at least so it looked. "Sweetie pie" brings back the façade that must be scratched away.

It was a faux-pas.

"Maman."

"Yes, I know, excuse me. No sweetie pie talk, Clara. We're tired, tense, both of us. We're going to talk about shocking, inappropriate things. You see, right from the start, it's difficult. We have two solutions. Either we think too much, walk on eggshells, tiptoe along, move in tiny increments. Or we dive in head-first and to hell with whatever we say. In any case, they'll never be the right words. Never. Because there are no words for this. So I propose we dive in. What do you want to know, Clara? How your father died? I have no idea, no one knows, no one will ever know. I too have trouble with the theory that it was a mere accident, all alone, on a straight road, on a night when the weather was good, with no evidence of braking.

He'd been drinking, he was under pressure, no doubt worried about work. And clearly about my having left. But that did not really change much for him; we were so removed from one another. I don't know if he didn't care about it or if it weighed on him. But it doesn't matter. That night, he lost control, he killed himself. Period. We're going to stick to this version for both of our sakes. I can tell what you think, and I also wondered about suicide, but let's just please agree to never know.

"Maman."

"Yes, you're right, I'm the only one talking. What else do you want to know? Is it about the letters? Did you find them? Read them? I know you cleaned up when you got here that night, thank you for that. Is that what you want us to talk about? I wrote it all down, I have nothing to add. The rest is between your father and me."

"Maman, please! Dive right in, sure, but it can't be one-sided!"

Clara had been waiting to have an adult discussion

with her mother, not for her to pull out her childhood nickname, from which she'd been gradually distancing herself. And she was certainly not ready for some apologetic monologue.

"Try and listen Maman. I've thought long and hard, day and night. Night and night, above all. I've thought about the accident. I tried to figure it out, and it's true I blamed you, for having harassed him, pushed him over the edge. I thought about other causes; I imagined going to the police to tell them my suspicions. What if someone had tampered with his car, what if someone hated him that much, and who, and why? And of course I found answers and names for all of my theories. But I'm through with nocturnal ravings. It's over, Maman, I agree with you, we'll never know and it's no doubt for the better. But since the two of us are here..."

Béatrice sits up in the armchair.

"What else then?"

The words come out a bit too harshly, drier that she would have wanted them to.

"Why did you stay?"

OK. Now Clara has spat it out.

For Béatrice, the hardest part has begun. Convincing her daughter that she was very young, that she did not immediately understand that she had been the victim of a hideous act. Or that she understood, but that she felt guilty, terribly guilty, and ashamed at the same time because Gaëtan, apart from that night, was an amazing, sweet, funny, caring guy. She'd been torn between the shame of what had happened in her body and the shame of accusing him. He was so perfect, while she was guilty of allowing it to happen, guilty of having perhaps brought it on herself.

And he was so charming, and the months passed by. And then there was Clara and their life together, the three of them. Her shame stayed hidden away in a minuscule corner, lying in ambush. Then their relationship had grown listless. And there were the more recent reverberations of Gaëtan's behavior. With increasingly precise facts, evidence. And then Virginie began to speak up too. And she finally saw Gaëtan's true colors. The shame came back, but it was doubled with anger this time.

She was ashamed of not having said anything, done anything. As she waited to end all those years of lies and impunity with the help of the police, and later the court, Béatrice just had to write to Gaëtan. Day after day, so he'd become addicted to her letters. So she could possess him in her turn.

What she will have trouble articulating can nevertheless be said in very few words: she actually knew everything would end badly, from the start.

The shame, the blame, the naïveté, the seduction, the fact that Clara needed parents. All the words Béatrice has just uttered form an incomplete explanation. A lie by omission. The time has come to read the last letter to her daughter, the one that was never mailed and that she keeps in her handbag. A post-mortem letter dated June 25th which states her years-long determination. Which states her intention to find, in the forest of her murdered youth, a tree, against which a car could crash. However lightly it's pushed—even if indirectly.

EARLY MORNING, JUNE 25,

GAËTAN,

Clara just called me.

So you will not be reading my letters anymore. I'll continue to write to you. For no reason, or for myself. I'll pursue this one-sided correspondence. Will things be a bit calmer with the passing of time?

You've just scored a decisive point in your attempts to make me seem guilty. I'm defending myself, I will defend myself, and you will not silence me. Putting down my pen would be celebrating your victory. You have chosen to no longer read my words. Go right ahead.

Clara told me everything. About the car, the speed, your blood alcohol level. And that tree in the Verdon Forest. At the wrong place, at the wrong time, like me, thirty-two years earlier, almost to the day. Yet what were you doing last night, in such fancy clothes in the middle of the forest? Did you really think that Virginie and I were going to come and meet you to celebrate our filing the complaint with the police, our meetings with the attorney, our ferocious determination to see everything through? And what a state you'd gotten yourself into! Too much pressure, too much fear, panic to the point of losing your faculties? You poor idiot!

• • •

Here I am, certain that you've read all of my letters—there's now no mistaking that you were found on this road last night, precisely last night, June 24th, in formal attire. Since you played the game beyond my hopes, I'm going to share a secret with you that no one else will read. Why do you think I stayed with you for all those years? For your presence, your suits, your cash, your position, your name maybe? For Clara? A bit of all that, yes, no doubt. But Clara would have understood. Even your two pitiable friends, Freddy and Sten, who were with you that Saturday night in June 1990, would have understood why I was leaving. Just like that forest on the side of the road that keeps the memory of that group rape—at least the second one, since it seems Virginie had already suffered at your criminal hands. And yet, I stayed. For this precise moment. For this deadly encounter with a courageous oak tree.

Béatrice

acknowledgments

Books are born from stories and encounters. Then, as the writing process moves forward, incredible people turn up along the way.

There were many people who helped make *Sens Unique* a reality in France in 2024. I must of course thank Frédérique, for her sharp eye and support, and Michaël of L'Ire de l'Ours press.

They both know how much I'm indebted to them, but may these words serve to thank them once again.

For their encouragement and valuable feedback, many thanks to:

my family, naturally
my close friends,
my faithful readers, Philippe and Martine.

And to my favorite booksellers: Christel (who has played a huge part in my literary journey), Nadine (for her analytical, kind, and very supportive reading), as well as Marianne, Hélène, and Céline, who are passionate about words and books, and who do an incredible job sending stories out into the world.

To my Wednesday night writing friends: because

writing thrives as much on fits of laughter as those moments where time seems to stand still.

To everyone at Maison Gueffier, and Sophie and Éloïse in particular, who believe words should hold pride of place in a city.

To my town media library, which is a bit like a second home to me.

All of my gratitude to the team at Pro/p(r)ose Magazine (and Karen in particular), who have created such a lovely space for literature.

For having offered Béatrice the opportunity to cross the ocean, beyond borders and languages, I'd like to give special thanks to Liza—for everything.

The same goes for John, who believed in this story and welcomed it to Silent Clamor Press, with this beautiful cover.

Thank you François, for the foreword, and Jean-Luc, for the pencil drawings. Thank you both for your friendship, and for placing art at the center of our lives and our work. I am so honored to have you participate in this book.

And Philippe—for the words to live by.

Hélène

about the author

Hélène Hérault is a French writer and poet based in the Vendée. Her incisive poetry and prose draw on her life experiences as an activist, mother, grandmother, and voracious reader. Previous work includes the short story collection *La Petite Prigent,* winner of the 2018 Ozoir'Elles prize, and the short stories "Un Exil de Papier," awarded second prize in the 2019 Concours de Nouvelles LIRE-Librinova, and "Au Prix Fort," which appeared in the anthology *Loin du Coeur* (benefiting the Solidarité Femmes foundation). She is a frequent and long-standing contributor of poetry to *Pro/p(r)ose Magazine.* Her poetry has appeared in English (translated by Liza

Tripp) in both Cordite Poetry Review and the International Poetry Review.

about the translator

Liza Tripp has been a translator of French, Spanish, Italian and Portuguese into English texts since 2003. She has translated numerous books for publishers including Assouline, Rizzoli, and Schiffer Publishing, as well as *I'll Look Myself in the Eyes* by Rim Battal, published by Galiot Press. She holds an M.Phil. in French Translation from CUNY Graduate Center, a B.A. in French Translation from Barnard College, and a Certificate in French to English Translation from New York University. She can be found at www.lizatripp.com and @lizatripp.

At Silent Clamor Press, we seek to illuminate the human experience with excitement, elegance, and unflinching honesty. If this work has resonated with you—offering a profound journey or a new way of seeing the world—consider sharing your reflections with others. Your voice enriches the ongoing conversation that keeps literature vital and transformative.

www.ingramcontent.com/pod-product-compliance
Lightning Source LLC
Chambersburg PA
CBHW030540130726
48054CB00020B/113

* 9 7 8 1 9 7 1 2 3 8 9 9 9 *